William Henry Rawle

Unveiling of the Statue of Chief Justice Marshall

At Washington, May 10th, 1884

William Henry Rawle

Unveiling of the Statue of Chief Justice Marshall
At Washington, May 10th, 1884

ISBN/EAN: 9783337381127

Printed in Europe, USA, Canada, Australia, Japan

Cover: Foto ©Andreas Hilbeck / pixelio.de

More available books at **www.hansebooks.com**

UNVEILING OF THE STATUE

OF

CHIEF JUSTICE MARSHALL,

AT

WASHINGTON, MAY 10th, 1884.

ORATION

BY

WILLIAM HENRY RAWLE, LL. D.

PHILADELPHIA:
ALLEN, LANE & SCOTT'S PRINTING HOUSE,
229-231 South Fifth Street.
1884.

JOHN MARSHALL, CHIEF JUSTICE OF THE UNITED STATES, has been dead for nearly half a century, and if it be asked why at this late day we have come together to do tardy justice to his memory and unveil this statue in his honour, the answer may be given in a few words. The history dates from his death. He had held his last Court, and had come Northward to seek medical aid in the city of Philadelphia, and there, on the 6th of July, 1835, he died. While tributes of respect for the man and of grief for the national loss were paid throughout the country, it was felt by the Bar of the city where he died that a lasting monument should be erected to his memory in the capital of the nation. To this end subscriptions, limited in amount, were asked. About half came from the Bar of Philadelphia, and of the rest, the largest contribution was from the city of Richmond, but all told, the sum was utterly insufficient. What money there was, was invested by trustees as "The Marshall Memorial Fund," and then the matter seemed to pass out of men's minds. Nearly fifty years went on. Another generation and still another came into the world, till lately, on the death of the survivor of the trustees, himself an old man, the late Peter McCall, the almost-forgotten fund was found to have been increased, by honest stewardship, seven fold. Of the original subscribers but six were known to be alive, and upon their application trustees were appointed to apply the fund to its original purpose. It happened that at this time the Forty-seventh Congress appropriated of the people's money a sum about equal in amount for the erection of a statue to the memory of Chief Justice Marshall, to be "placed in a suitable public reservation in the city of Washington." To serve their common purpose, the Congressional committee and the trustees agreed to unite in the erection of a statue and pedestal; and after much thought and care the commission was intrusted to William W. Story, an artist who brought to the task not only his acknowledged genius, but a keen desire to perpetuate through the work of his hands the face and form of one who had been not only his father's professional brother but the object of his chiefest respect and admiration. That work now stands before you. Its pedestal bears the simple inscription:—

JOHN MARSHALL

CHIEF JUSTICE OF THE UNITED STATES

ERECTED BY

THE BAR AND THE CONGRESS

OF THE UNITED STATES

A. D. MDCCCLXXXIV.

No more "suitable public reservation" could be found than the ground on which we stand, almost within the shadow of the capitol in which for more than thirty years he held the highest judicial position in the country.

It may well be that the even tenour of his judicial life has driven from some minds the story of his brilliant and eventful youth. The same simplicity, the same modesty which marked the child distinguished the great Chief Justice, but, as a Judge, his life was necessarily one of thought and study, of enforced retirement from much of the busy world, dealing more with results than processes; and the surges of faction and of passion, the heat of ambition, the thirst of power reached him not in his high judicial station. Yet he had himself been a busy actor on the scenes of life, and if his later days seemed colourless, the story of his earlier years is full of charm.

The eldest. of a large family, reared in Fauquier county, in Virginia, he was one of the tenderest, the most lovable of children; he had never, said his father, seriously displeased him in his life. To his mother, to his sisters especially, did he bear that chivalrous devotion which to the last hour of his life he showed to women. Such education as came to him was little got from schools, for the thinly-settled country and his father's limited means forbade this. A year's Latin at fourteen at a school a hundred miles from his home and another year's Latin at home with the rector of the parish was the sum of his classical teaching. What else of it he learned was with the unsympathetic aid of grammar and dictionary. But his father—who Marshall was wont to say was a far abler man than any of his sons, and who in early life was Washington's companion as a land-surveyor, and, later, fought gallantly under him—his father was well read in English literature, and loved to open its treasures to the quick, receptive mind of his eldest child, who in it all, especially in history and still more in poetry, found an enduring delight. Much of his time was passed in the open air, among the hills and valleys of that beautiful country, and thus it was that in active exercise, in day dreams of heroism and poetry, in rapid and eager mastery of such learning as came within his reach, and surrounded by the tender love, the idolatry of a happy family, his earlier days were passed.

The first note of war that rang through the land called him to arms, and from 1775, when was his first battle on the soil of his own State, until the end of 1779, he was in the army. Through the battles of Iron Hill, of Brandywine, of Germantown and of Monmouth, he bore himself bravely, and through the dreary privations, the hunger and the nakedness of that ghastly winter at Valley Forge, his patient endurance and his cheeriness bespoke the very sweetest temper that ever man was blessed with. So long as any lived to speak, men would tell how he was loved by the soldiers and by his brother officers; how he was the arbiter of their differences and the composer of their disputes, and when called to act, as he often was, as judge advocate, he exercised that peculiar and delicate judgment required of him who is not only the prosecutor but the protector of the accused. It was in the duties of this office that he first met and came to know well the two men whom of all others on earth he most admired and loved and whose impress he bore through his life, Washington and Hamilton.

While of Marshall's life, war was but the brief opening episode, yet before we leave these days, one part of them has a peculiar charm. There were more officers than were needed, and he had come back to his home. His letters from camp had been read with delight by his sisters and his sisters' friends. His reputation as a soldier had preceded him, and the daughters of Virginia, then, as ever, ready to welcome those who do service to the State, greeted him with their sweetest smiles. One of these was a shy, diffident girl of fourteen; and to the amazement of all, and perhaps to her own, from that time his devotion to her knew no variableness neither shadow of turning. She afterwards became his wife, and for fifty years, in sickness and in health, he loved and cherished her till, as he himself said, " her sainted spirit fled from the sufferings of life." When her release came at last, he mourned her as he had loved her, and the years were few before he followed her to the grave.

But from this happy home he tore himself away, and at the college of William and Mary attended a course of law lectures and in due time was admitted to practice. But practice there was none, for Arnold had then invaded Virginia and it was literally true that *inter arma silent leges*. To resist the invasion, Marshall returned to the army, and at its end, there being still a redundance of officers in the Virginia line, he resigned his commission and again took up his studies. With the return of peace the courts were opened and his career at the bar began. Tradition tells how even at that early day his characteristic traits began to show themselves—his simple, quiet bearing, his frankness and candour, his marvellous grasp of principle, his power of clear statement and his logical reasoning. It is pleasant to know that his rapid rise excited no envy among his associates, for his other high qualities were exceeded by his modesty. In after life, this modesty was wont to attribute his success to the "too partial regard of his former companions-in-arms, who, at the end of the war had returned to their families and were scattered over the States." But the cause was in himself, and not in his friends.

In the spring of 1782, he was elected to the State Legislature, and in the autumn chosen to the Executive Council. In the next year took place his happy marriage, his removal to Richmond, thenceforth his home, and soon after, his retirement, as he supposed, from public life. But this was not to be, for his election again and again to the legislature, called on him for service which he was too patriotic to withhold, even had he felt less keenly how full of trouble were the times. Marshall threw himself, heart and soul, into the great questions which bade fair to destroy by dissension what had been won by arms, and opposed to the best talent of his own State, he ranged himself with an unpopular minority. In measured words, years later, when he wrote the life of Washington, he defined the issue which then threatened to tear the country asunder. It was, he said, "divided into two great political parties, the one of which contemplated America as a nation, and labored incessantly to invest the Federal head with powers competent to the preservation of the Union. The other attached itself to the State government, viewed all the powers of Congress with jealousy, and assented reluctantly to measures which would enable the head to act in any respect independently of the members." Though the proposed Constitution might form, as its preamble declares, "a more perfect union" than had the Articles of Confederation; though it might prevent anarchy and save the States from becoming secret or open enemies of each other; though it might replace "a government depending upon thirteen distinct sovereignties for the preservation of the public faith" by one whose power might regulate and control them all—the more numerous and powerful, and certainly the more clamorous party insisted that such evils, and evils worse than these, were as nothing compared to the surrender of State independence to Federal sovereignty. In public and private, in popular meetings, in legislatures and in conventions, on both sides passion was mingled with argument. Notably in Marshall's own State did many of her ablest sons, then and afterwards most dear to her, throw all that they had of courage, of high character and of patriotism, into the attempt to save the young country from its threatened yoke of despotism. Equally brave and able were those few who led the other party, and chief among them were Washington, Madison, Randolph and, later, Marshall. Young as he was, it was felt that such a man could not be left out of the State convention to which the Constitution was to be submitted, but he was warned by his best friends that unless he should pledge himself to oppose it his defeat was certain. He said plainly that, if elected, he should be "a determined advocate for its adoption," and his integrity and fearlessness overcame even the prejudices of his constituents. And in that memorable debate, which lasted five-and-twenty days, though with his usual modesty he contented himself with supporting the lead of Madison, three times he came to the front, and to the questions of the power of taxation, the power over the militia and the power of the judiciary, he brought the full force of his fast developing strength. The contest was severe and the vote close. The Constitution was ratified by a majority of only ten. But as to Marshall, it has been truly said that "in sustaining the Constitution, he unconsciously prepared for his own glory the imperishable connection which his name now has with its principles." And again his modesty would have it that he builded better than he knew, for in later times he would ascribe the course which he took to casual circumstances as much as to judgment; he had early, he said, caught up the words, " united we stand, divided we fall;" the feelings they inspired became a part of his being; he carried them into the army where, associating with brave men from different States who were risking life and all else in a common cause, he was confirmed in the habit of considering America as his country, and Congress as his government.

The convention was held in 1788. Again Marshall was sent to the legislature, where in power of logical debate he confessedly led the House, until in 1792 he left it finally.

During the next five years he was at the height of his professional reputation. The Federal reports and those of his own State show that among a bar distinguished almost beyond all others, he was engaged in most of the important cases of the time. A few of these he has reported himself; they are modestly inserted at the end of the volume, and are referred to by the reporter as contributed "by a gentleman high in practice at the time and by whose permission they are now published."

And here a word must be said as to the nature and extent of his technical learning, for it is almost without parallel that one should admittedly have held the highest position at the bar, and then for thirty-five years should, as admittedly, have held the reputation of a great judge, when the entire time between the very commencement of his studies and his relinquishment of practice was less than seventeen years. In that generation of lawyers and the generation which succeeded them, it was not unusual that more than half that time passed before they had either a cause or a client. Marshall had emphatically what is called a legal mind; his marvellous instinct as to what the law *ought* to be doubtless saved him much labour which was necessary to those less intellectually great. With the principles of the science he was of course familiar; with their sources he was scarcely less so. A century ago there was less law to be learned and men learned it more completely. Except as to such addition as has of late years come to us from the civil law, the foundation of it was the same as now—the same common law, the same decisions, the same statutes—and in that day, a century's separation from the mother country had wrought little change in the colonies except to adapt this law to their local needs with marvellous skill. Save as to this, the law of the one country was the law of the other, and the decisions at Westminster Hall before the Revolution were of as much authority here as there. There was not a single published volume of American reports. The enormous superstructure which has since been raised upon the same foundation, bewildering from its height, the number of its stories, the vast number of its chambers, the intricacies of its passages, has been a necessity from the growth of a country rapid beyond precedent in a century to which history knows no parallel. But the foundation of it was the same, and the men of the last century had not far to go beyond the foundation, and hence their technical learning was, as to some at least, more complete, if not more profound. There were a few who said that Marshall was never what is called a thoroughly technical lawyer. If by this is meant that he never mistook the grooves and ruts of the law for the law itself—that he looked at the law from above and not from below, and did not cite precedent where citation was not necessary—the remark might have semblance of truth, but the same might be said of his noted abstinence from illustration and analogy, both of which he could, upon occasion, call in aid; but no one can read those arguments at the bar or judgments on the bench in which he thought it needful to establish his propositions by technical precedents, without feeling that he possessed as well the knowledge of their existence and the reason of their existence, as the power to analyze them. But he never mistook the means for the end.

Even in the height of his prosperous labour he never turned his back upon public duty. Not all the excesses of the French revolution could make the mass of Americans forget that France had been our ally in the war with England, and when in 1793 these nations took arms against each other, and our Proclamation of Neutrality was issued to the world, loud and deep were the curses that rang through the land. Hated as the proclamation was, Marshall had no doubt of its wisdom. Great was his grief to oppose himself to the judgment of Madison, but he was content to share the odium heaped upon Hamilton and Washington, and to be denounced as an aristocrat, a loyalist and an enemy to republicanism. With rare courage, at a public meeting at Richmond he defended the wisdom and policy of the administration, and his argument as to the constitutionality of the proclamation anticipated the judgment of the world.

Two years later came a severer trial. Without his knowledge and against his will, Marshall had been again elected to the legislature. Our minister to Great Britain had concluded a commercial treaty with that power, and its ratification had been advised by the Senate and acted on by the President. The indignation of the people knew no bounds. In no State was it greater than in Virginia. The treaty was "Insulting to the dignity, injurious to the interests, dangerous to the security and repugnant to the Constitution of the United States"—so said the resolutions of a remarkable meeting at Richmond, and these words echoed through the country. Had not the Constitution given to Congress the right to regulate commerce, and how dared the executive, without Congress, negotiate a treaty of commerce? Marshall's friends begged him, for his own sake, not to stem the popular torrent. He hoped at first that his own legislature might, as he wrote to Hamilton from Richmond, "ultimately consult the interest or honour of the nation. But now," he went on to say, "when all hope of this had vanished, it was deemed advisable to make the experiment, however hazardous it might be. A meeting was called which was more numerous than I have ever seen at this place ; and after a very ardent and zealous discussion, which consumed the day, a decided majority declared in favor of a resolution that the welfare and honour of the nation required us to give full effect to the treaty negotiated with Britain." Thus measuredly he told the story of one of his greatest triumphs, and afterwards, in his place in the House, he again met the constitutional objection in a speech which, men said at the time, was even stronger than the other. As he spoke, reason asserted her sway over passion, party feeling gave way to conviction, and for once the vote of the House was turned. Of this speech no recorded trace remains, but even in that time when news travelled slowly its fame spread abroad, and the subsequent conduct of every administration has to this day rested upon the construction then given to the Constitution by Marshall.

Henceforth his reputation became national, and when a few months later he came to Philadelphia to argue the great case of the confiscation by Virginia of the British debts, a contemporary said of him, "Speaking, as he always does, to the judgment merely and for the simple purpose of convincing, he was justly pronounced one of the greatest men in the country." He were less than human not to be moved by this, but in writing to a friend, he modestly said, "A Virginian who supported with any sort of reputation the measures of the government, was such a *rara avis* that I was received with a degree of kindness which I had not anticipated." Soon after, Washington offered him the office of Attorney-General, and some months later, the mission to France. Both he declined. His determination to remain at the bar was, he thought, unalterable.

And again he altered it. Neither France herself nor the "French patriots" here had forgotten or forgiven the treaty with Great Britain, and if the disgust at our persistent neutrality did not break into open war, it was because France knew, or thought she knew, that the entire American opposition to the government was on her side. Just short of war she stopped. Privateers fitted out by orders of the French minister here preyed upon our commerce; the very ship which brought him to our shores began to capture our vessels before even his credentials had been presented; later, by order of the Directory he suspended his diplomatic functions here and flung to our people turgid words of bitterness as he left; the minister whom we had sent to France when Marshall had declined to go, was not only not received, but was ordered out of the country and threatened with the police. The crisis required the greatest wisdom and firmness which the country could command. Mr. Adams was then President; he never lacked firmness, and his words to Congress at its special session were full of fearless dignity. Three envoys, said he, "persons of talents and integrity, long known and intrusted in the three great divisions of the Union," were to be sent to France, and Marshall was to be one of them. It went hard with him but the struggle was short, and as he left his home at Richmond crowds of citizens attended him for miles, and all party feeling was merged in respect and affection. The issue of his errand belongs to history. He has himself told us, in his Life of Washington, how the envoys—his own name being characteristically withheld—were met by contumely and insult; how the wiliest minister of the age suggested that a large sum of money must be paid to the Directory as a mere preliminary to negotiation; how, if they refused, it would be known at home that they were corrupted by British influence, and how insults and menaces were borne with equal dignity. But he has not told us that his were the two letters to Talleyrand which have justly been regarded as among the ablest State papers in diplomacy. They were unanswerable, and nothing remained but to get Marshall and one of his colleagues out of the country with as little delay as was consistent with additional marks of contempt. His return showed that republics are not always ungrateful, for there came out to him on his arrival a crowd even greater than that which had witnessed his departure, the Secretary of State and other officials among them, and at a celebration in his honour the phrase was coined which afterwards became national, " Millions for defence, but not one cent for tribute."

Now surely he had earned the right to return to his loved professional labour. Nor only this—he had earned the right to such honour as the dignified labour of high judicial station could alone afford. The position of Justice of the Supreme Court of the United States had fallen vacant, and the President's choice rested on Marshall. " He has raised the American people in their own esteem," wrote Mr. Adams to the Secretary of State, "and if the influence of truth and justice, reason and argument, is not lost in Europe, he has raised the consideration of the United States in that quarter." But again there had come to him the call of duty. For Washington, who, in view of the expected war with France, had been appointed to command the army, had begged Marshall to come to him at Mount Vernon, and there in earnest talk for days dwelt upon the importance to the country that he should be returned to Congress. His reluctance was great not only to re-enter public life but to throw himself into a contest sure to be marked with an intensity of public excitement, degenerating into private calumny. If Washington himself had not escaped this, how should he ?

The canvass began. In the midst of it came the offer of the repose and dignity of the Supreme Bench. But his word had been given, and he at once declined. The contest was severe, his majority was small, and his election, though intensely grateful to Washington and those who thought with him, was met with many misgivings from some who thought him "too much disposed to govern the world according to rules of logic."

His first act in Congress was to announce the death of Washington, and the words of the resolutions which he then presented, though written by another, meet our eyes on every hand, "First in war, first in peace, and first in the hearts of his countrymen." It was like Marshall that when, later, he came to write the life of Washington, he should have said that the resolutions were presented by "a member of the House."

In that House—the last Congress that sat in Philadelphia—he met the ablest men of the country. New member as he was, when the debate involved questions of law or the Constitution, he was confessedly the first man in it. His speech on the question of Nash's surrender is said to be the only one ever revised by him, and, as it stands, is a model of parliamentary argument. The President had advised the surrender of the prisoner to the English government to answer a charge of murder on the high seas on board a British man-of-war. Popular outcry insisted that the prisoner was an American, unlawfully impressed, and that the death was caused in his attempt to regain his freedom, and though this was untrue, it was urged that as the case involved principles of law, the question of surrender was one for judicial and not executive decision. In most of its aspects the subject was confessedly new, but it was exhausted by Marshall. Not every case, he showed, which involves principles of law necessarily came before the courts; the parties here were two nations, who could not litigate their claims; the demand was not a case for judicial cognizance; the treaty under which the surrender was made was a law enjoining the performance of a particular object; the department to perform it was the Executive, who, under the Constitution, was to "take care that the laws be faithfully executed;" and even if Congress had not yet prescribed the particular mode by which this was to be done, it was not the less the duty of the Executive to execute it by any means it then possessed.

There was no answer to this, worthy the name; the member selected to answer it sat silent; the resolutions against the Executive were lost, and thus the power was lodged where it should belong, and an unwelcome and inappropriate jurisdiction diverted from the Judiciary.

The session was just over, when, in May, the President, without consulting Marshall, appointed him Secretary of War. He wrote to decline. As part of the well-known disruption of the Cabinet, the office of Secretary of State became vacant, and Marshall was appointed to and accepted it. During his short tenure of office, an occasion arose for the display of his best powers, in his dispatch to our minister to England concerning questions of great moment under our treaty, of contraband, blockade, impressment, and compensation to British subjects, a State paper not surpassed by any in the archives of that Department.

The autumn of 1800 witnessed the defeat of Mr. Adams for the Presidency and the resignation of Chief Justice Ellsworth, and, at Marshall's suggestion, Chief Justice Jay was invited to return to his former position, but declined. On being again consulted, Marshall urged the appointment of Mr. Justice Patterson, then on the Supreme Bench. Some said that the vacant office might possibly be filled by the President himself after the 3d of March, but Mr. Adams disclaimed the idea. "I have already," wrote he, "by the nomination to this office of a gentleman in full vigor of middle life, in the full habits of business, and whose reading in the science of law is fresh in his head, put it wholly out of my power, and indeed it never was in my hopes and wishes," and on the 31st of January, 1801, he requested the Secretary of War "to execute the office of Secretary of State so far as to affix the seal of the United States to the enclosed commission to the present Secretary of State, John Marshall of Virginia, to be Chief Justice of the United States." He was then forty-six years old.

It is difficult for the present generation to appreciate the contrast between the Supreme Court to which Marshall came and the Supreme Court as he left it; the contrast is scarcely less between the Court as he left it and the Court of to-day. For the first time in the history of the world had a written constitution become an organic law of government; for the first time was such an instrument to be submitted to judgment. With admirable force Mr. Gladstone has said, " As the British Constitution is the most subtile organism which has proceeded from progressive history, so the American Constitution is the most wonderful work ever struck off at a given time by the brain and purpose of man." On that subtile and unwritten Constitution of England, the professional training of every older lawyer in the country had been based, and they had learned from it that the power of Parliament was above and beyond the judgments of any court in the realm. Though this American Constitution declared in so many words that the judicial power should extend to "all cases arising under the Constitution and the laws of the United States," yet it was difficult for men so trained to conceive how any law which the Legislative department might pass and the Executive approve could be set aside by the mere judgment of a court. There was no precedent for it in ancient or modern history. Hence when first this question was suggested in a Federal court, it was received with grave misgiving; the general principles of the Constitution were not, it was said, to be regarded as rules to fetter and control, but as matter merely declaratory and directory; and even if legislative acts directly contrary to it *should* be void, whose was the power to declare them so?

Equally without precedent was every other question. Those who, in their places as legislators, had fought the battle of State sovereignty, were ready to urge in the courts of justice that the Federal Government could claim no powers that had not been delegated to it *in ipsissimis verbis*. If delegated at all, they were to be contracted by construction within the narrowest limits. Whether the right of Congress to pass all laws " necessary and proper " for the Federal Government was not restricted to such as were indispensable to that end; whether the right of taxation could be exercised by a State against creations of the Federal Government; whether a Federal court could revise the judgment of a State court in a case arising under the Constitution and laws of the United States; whether the officers of the Federal Government could be protected against State interference; how far extended the power of Congress to regulate commerce within the States; how far to regulate foreign commerce as against State enactment; how far extended the prohibition to the States against emitting bills of credit—these and like questions were absolutely without precedent.

It is not too much to say that but for Marshall such questions could hardly have been solved as they were. There have been great judges before and since, but none had ever such opportunity, and none ever seized and improved it as he did. For as was said by our late President, " He found the Constitution paper, and he made it power ; he found it a skeleton, and clothed it with flesh and blood." Not in a few feeble words at such a time as this can be told how, with easy power he grasped the momentous questions as they arose ; how his great statemanship lifted them to a high plane ; how his own clear vision pierced clouds which caused others to see as through a glass darkly, and how all that his wisdom could conceive and his reason could prove was backed by a judicial courage unequalled in history.

It may be doubted whether, great as is his reputation, full justice has yet been done him. In his interpretation of the law, the premises seem so undeniable, the reasoning so logical, the conclusions so irresistible, that men are wont to wonder that there had ever been any question at all.

A single instance—the first which arose—may tell its own story. Congress had given to his own court a jurisdiction not within the range of its powers under the Constitution. If it could lawfully do this, the case before the court was plain. Whether it could, said the court, in Marshall's words, "Whether an act repugnant to the Constitution can become the law of the land, is a question deeply interesting to the United States, but, happily, not of an intricacy proportioned to its interest;" and in these few words was the demonstration made: "It is a proposition too plain to be contested, that the Constitution controls any legislative act repugnant to it, or that the legislature can alter the Constitution by an ordinary act. Between these alternatives there is no middle ground. The Constitution is either a superior paramount law, unchangeable by ordinary means, or it is on a level with ordinary legislative acts, and, like other acts, is alterable when the legislature shall please to alter it. If the former part of the alternative be true, then a legislative act contrary to the Constitution is not law ; if the latter part be true, then written constitutions are absurd attempts on the part of the people to limit a power in its own nature illimitable."

Here was established one of the great foundation principles of the government, and then in a few sentences, and for the first time, was clearly and tersely stated the theory of the Constitution as to the separate powers of the Legislature and the Judiciary. If, he said, its theory was that an act of the Legislature repugnant to it was void, such an act could not bind the courts and oblige them to give it effect. This would be to overthrow in fact what was established in theory. It was of the very essence of judicial duty to expound and interpret the law; to determine which of two conflicting laws should prevail. When a law came in conflict with the Constitution, the judicial department must decide between them. Otherwise, the courts must close their eyes on the Constitution, which they were sworn to support, and see only the law.

The exposition thus begun was continued for more than thirty years, and in a series of judgments, contained in many volumes, is to be found the basis of what is to-day the constitutional law of this country. Were it possible, it would be inappropriate to follow here, with whatever profit, the processes by which this great work was done. The least approach to technical analysis would demand a statement of the successive questions as they arose, each fraught with the history of the time and each suggesting illustrations and analogies which subsequent time has developed. It may have been that could Marshall have foreseen the extent to which, in some instances, his conclusions could be carried, in the uncertain future and under such wholly changed circumstances as no man could then conjecture, he would possibly have qualified or limited their application; but the marvel is, that of all he wrought in the field of constitutional labour there is so little that admits of even question.

But besides this, there was much more. It has been truly said of him that he would have been a great judge at any time and in any country. Great in the sense in which Nottingham and Hardwicke as to equity, were great; in which

Mansfield as to commercial law and Stowell as to admiralty, were great—great in that, with little precedent to guide them, they produced a system with which the wisdom of succeeding generations has found little fault and has little changed. In Marshall's court there was little precedent by which to determine the rights of the Indian tribes over the land which had once been theirs, or their rights as nations against the States in which they dwelt; there was little precedent when, beyond the seas, the heat of war had produced the British Orders in Council and the retaliatory Berlin and Milan Decrees; when the conflicting rights of neutrals and belligerents, of captors and claimants, of those trading under the flag of peace and those privateering under letters of marque and reprisal; when the effect of the judgments of foreign tribunals; when the jurisdiction of the sovereign upon the high seas—when these and similar questions arose, there was little precedent for their solution, and they had to be considered upon broad and general principles of jurisprudence, and the result has been a code for future time.

Passing from this, a word must be said as to his judicial conduct when sitting apart from his brethren in his Circuit Courts. Especially when presiding over trials by jury his best personal characteristics were shown; the dignity, maintained without effort, which forbade the possibility of unseemly difference, the quick comprehension, the unfailing patience, the prompt ruling, the serene impartiality and, when required, the most absolute courage and independence made up as nearly perfect a judge at Nisi Prius as the world has ever known.

One instance only can be noticed here. The story of Aaron Burr, with all its reality and all its romance, must always, spite of much that is repugnant, fascinate both young and old. When in a phase of his varied life, he who had been noted, if not famous, as a soldier, as a lawyer, as an orator, who had won the reason of men and charmed the hearts of women, who had held the high office of Vice-President of the United States, and whose hands were red with the blood of Hamilton—when he found himself on trial for his life upon the charge of high treason, before a judge who was Hamilton's dear friend and a jury chosen with difficulty from an excited people, what wonder that, like Cain, he felt himself singled out from his fellows, and coming between his counsel and the court, exclaimed : "Would to God that I did stand on the same ground with any other man !" And yet the impartiality which marked the conduct of those trials was never excelled in history. By the law of our mother country to have only compassed and imagined the government's subversion was treason ; but, according to our Constitution, "treason against the United States shall consist only in levying war against them, or in adhering to their enemies, giving them aid and comfort," and can it be, said Marshall, that the landing of a few men, however desperate and however intent to overthrow the government of a State, was a levying of war ? It might be a conspiracy, but it was not treason within the Constitution—and Burr's accomplices were discharged of their high crime. And upon his own memorable trial—that strange scene in which these men, the prisoner and the judge, each so striking in appearance, were confronted, and as people said, " two such pairs of eyes had never looked into one another before "—upon that trial the scales of justice were held with absolutely even hand.

No greater display of judicial skill and judicial rectitude was ever witnessed. No more effective dignity ever added weight to judicial language. Outside the court and through the country it was cried that "the people of America demanded a conviction," and within it all the pressure which counsel dared to borrow was exerted to this end. It could hardly be passed by. "That this court dares not usurp power, is most true," began the last lines of Marshall's charge to the jury. "That this court dares not shrink from its duty, is not less true. No man is desirous of becoming the peculiar subject of calumny. No man, might he let the bitter cup pass from him without self-reproach, would drain it to the bottom. But if he have no choice in the case, if there be no alternative presented to him but a dereliction of duty or the opprobrium of those who are denominated the world, he merits the contempt as well as the indignation of his country, who can hesitate which to embrace." That counsel should, he said, be impatient at any deliberation of the court, and suspect or fear the operation of motives to which alone they could ascribe that deliberation, was perhaps a frailty incident to human nature, "but if any conduct could warrant a sentiment that it would deviate to the one side or the other from the line prescribed by duty and by law, that conduct would be viewed by the judges themselves with an eye of extreme severity, and would long be recollected with deep and serious regrets."

The result was acquittal, and as was said by the angry counsel for the Government, "Marshall has stepped in between Burr and death!" Though the disappointment was extreme; though starting from the level of excited popular feeling, it made its way upward till it reached the dignity of grave dissatisfaction expressed in a President's message to Congress; though the trial led to legislative alteration of the law, the judge was unmoved by criticism, no matter from what quarter, and was content to await the judgment of posterity that never, in all the dark history of State trials, was the law, as then it stood and bound both parties, ever interpreted with more impartiality to the accuser and the accused.

Once only did Marshall enter the field of authorship. Washington had bequeathed all his papers, public and private, to his favourite nephew, who was one of Marshall's associates on the bench. It was agreed between them that Judge Washington should contribute the material and that Marshall should prepare the biography. The bulk of papers was enormous, and Marshall had just taken his seat on the bench and was deep in judicial work. The task was done under severe pressure, and ill health more than once interrupted it; but it was a labour of love, and his whole heart went out toward the subject. His political opponents feared that his strong convictions, which he never concealed, would now be turned to the account of his party, but the writer was as impartial as the judge. He recalled and perpetuated the intrigues and cabals, the disappointments and the griefs which, equally with the successes, were part of Washington's life; but full justice was done to those men whom both Washington and his biographer distrusted and opposed. It is agreed that for minuteness, impartiality and accuracy, the history is exceeded by none. There were those who said the work was colourless, and others were severe by reason of the absolute truth which became their most absolute punishment, but no one's judgment was as severe as Marshall's own, save only as to its accuracy. Once only was this seriously questioned, and by one of the most distinguished of his opponents, and the result was complete vindication.

It is matter of history that upon Washington's death the House had resolved that a marble monument should be erected in the city of Washington, " so designed as to commemorate the great events of his military and political life." But, as Marshall tells us, " that those great events should be commemorated could not be pleasing to those who had condemned, and continued to condemn, the whole course of his administration." The resolution was postponed in the Senate and never passed, and almost the only tinge of bitterness in his pages is that those who possessed the ascendency over the public sentiment employed their influence " to impress the idea that the only proper monument to a meritorious citizen was that which the people would erect in their affections." This he wrote in 1807 and repeated in 1832, and in the next year the people resolved that this should no longer be. The National Monument Association was then formed, and Marshall was its first president. Under its auspices, and with the aid, long after, of large appropriations by Congress, the gigantic column within our sight is slowly and gradually being reared.

Near the close of his life, when he was seventy-four years old, Marshall was chosen a member of the convention which met, in 1829, to revise the constitution of his native State. It was a remarkable body. The best men of the

State were there. Some of them were among the best men in the country, for then, as always, Virginia had been proud to rear and send forth men whose names were foremost in their country's history. Prominent among them were Madison, Monroe and Marshall. Even then, party spirit ran high. Two questions in particular, the basis of representation and the tenure of judicial office, distracted the convention, as they had distracted the people. On both these questions Marshall spoke with his accustomed dignity and not less than his accustomed force, and his words were listened to with reverent respect. Upon the subject of judicial tenure he spoke from his very heart, "with the fervour and almost the authority of an apostle." He knew, better than any, how a judge, standing between the powerful and the powerless, was bound to deal justice to both, and that to this end his own position should be beyond the reach of anything mortal. "The judicial department," said he, "comes home in its effects to every man's fireside; it passes on his property, his reputation, his life, his all. Is it not to the last degree important that he should be rendered perfectly and completely independent, with nothing to control him but God and his conscience?" And his next words were fraught with the wisdom of past ages, let us hope not with prophetic foreboding: "I have always thought, from my earliest youth till now, that the greatest scourge an angry Heaven ever inflicted upon an ungrateful and a sinning people, was an ignorant, a corrupt or a dependent judiciary."

Something has here been said of Marshall's inner life in its earlier years, and no man's life was ever more dear to those around him than was his from its beginning to its close. His singleness and simplicity of character, his simplicity of living, his love for the young and respect for the old, his deference to women, his courteous bearing, his tender charity, his reluctance to conceive offence and his readiness to forgive it, have become traditions from which in our memories of him we interweave all that we most look up to, with all that we take most nearly to our hearts.

As the evening of life cast its long shadows before him, the labour and sorrow that come with four-score years were not allowed to pass him by. Great physical suffering came to him ; the hours not absorbed in work brought to him memories of her whose life had been one with his for fifty years. The " great simple heart, too brave to be ashamed of tears," was too brave not to confess that rarely did he go through a night without shedding them for her. No outward trace of this betrayed itself, but lest some part of it should, all unconsciously to himself, impair his mental force, he begged those nearest to him to tell him in plain words when any signs of failing should appear. But the steady light within burned brightly to the last, however waning might be his mortal strength. He met his end, not at his home, but surrounded by those most dear to him. As it drew near, he wrote the simple inscription to be placed upon his grave. His parentage, his marriage, with his birth and death, were all he wished it to contain. And as the long summer day faded, the life of this great and good man went out, and in the words of his Church's liturgy, he was "gathered to his fathers, having the testimony of a good conscience, in the communion of the catholic Church, in the confidence of a certain faith, in the comfort of a reasonable, religious and holy hope, in favour with God and in perfect charity with the world."

And for what in his life he did for us, let there be lasting memory. He and the men of his time have passed away; other generations have succeeded them; other phases of our country's growth have come and gone; other trials, greater a hundred fold than he or they could possibly have imagined, have jeoparded the nation's life; but still that which they wrought remains to us, secured by the same means, enforced by the same authority, dearer far for all that is past, and holding together a great, a united and a happy people. And all largely because he whose figure is now before us has, above and beyond all others, taught the people of the United States, in words of absolute authority, what was the Constitution which they ordained, "in order to form a more perfect union, establish justice, insure domestic tranquillity, provide for the common defence, promote the general welfare, and secure the blessings of liberty to themselves and their posterity."

Wherefore with all gratitude, with fitting ceremony and circumstance; in the presence of the highest in the land; in the presence of those who make, of those who execute, and of those who interpret the laws; in the presence of those descendants in whose veins flows Marshall's blood, have the Bar and the Congress of the United States here set up this semblance of his living form, in perpetual memory of the honour, the reverence and the love which the people of his country bear to the great Chief Justice.

www.ingramcontent.com/pod-product-compliance
Lightning Source LLC
Chambersburg PA
CBHW030916260626
47169CB00008B/2881